Railway Series, No. 10

FOUR LITTLE ENGINES

by
THE REV. W. AWDRY

with illustrations by
C. REGINALD DALBY

KAYE & WARD LIMITED

First published by
Edmund Ward (Publishers) Ltd 1955
Ninth impression by Kaye & Ward Ltd
The Windmill Press, Kingswood, Tadworth, Surrey
1985

Copyright © 1955 Edmund Ward (Publishers) Ltd
Copyright © 1970 Kaye & Ward Ltd

ISBN 0 7182 0009 8

Printed and bound in Great Britain by
William Clowes Limited, Beccles and London

DEAR FRIENDS,

Sir Handel Brown is the owner of a little Railway which goes to Skarloey and Rheneas. Skarloey means "Lake in the Woods", and Rheneas means "Divided Waterfall". They are beautiful places, and lots of people visit them.

The Owner is very busy, so Mr Peter Sam, the Thin Controller, manages the railway.

The two Engines, who are called Skarloey and Rheneas, grew old and tired; so the Owner bought two others.

The stories tell you what happened.

THE AUTHOR

Skarloey Remembers

THE FAT CONTROLLER had sent Edward to the Works to be mended. Near the Works Station, Edward noticed a narrow-gauge engine standing in an open-sided shed.

"That's Skarloey," he thought, "what's he doing there?" He remembered Skarloey and his brother Rheneas, because in the old days he had often brought passengers who wanted to travel up to the Lake in their little train.

As the men at the Works could not mend him at once, Edward asked them to put him on a siding close to Skarloey.

Skarloey was pleased to see Edward.

"The Owner has just bought two more engines," he said.

"He told me I was a Very Old Engine, and deserved a good rest. He gave me this shed so that I could see everything and not be lonely. But I am lonely all the same," he continued sadly, "I miss Rheneas very much. Yesterday one of the new engines pushed him on a truck, and now he's gone to be mended.

"I wish I could be mended too, and pull coaches again."

"Have your coaches got names?" asked Edward.

"Oh, yes, there's Agnes, Ruth, Jemima, Lucy and Beatrice. Agnes is proud. She has cushions for first-class passengers. She pities Ruth, Jemima and Lucy, who are third-class with bare boards; but they all four sniff at Beatrice. Beatrice often smells of fish and cheese, but she is *most* important," said Skarloey earnestly, "she has a little window through which the Guard sells tickets. I sometimes leave the others behind, but I always take Beatrice. You *must* have tickets and a Guard you know."

"Of course," said Edward gravely.

"Rheneas and I," continued Skarloey, "used to take turns at pulling the trains. We know everybody, and everybody knows us. We whistle to the people in the fields, at level crossings, and in lonely cottages and farms, and the people always wave to us.

"We love passing the school playgrounds at break-time, for then the children will always run over to the fence to watch us go by. The passengers always wave, because they think the children are waving to them; but we engines know better, of course," said Skarloey importantly.

"Yes, we do indeed," agreed Edward.

"We take your tourists to the Lake and then get ready to pull the train back.

"We enjoy the morning journey home, because then our friends from the villages come down to do their shopping.

"We whistle before every station, 'Peep! Peeeep! Look out!' and the people are there ready.

" 'Where's Mrs Last?' asks the Guard.

" 'She's coming.'

" 'Peep peeeeep!' we whistle, and Mrs Last comes running on to the platform. 'We'll leave you behind one of these days, Missis,' laughs our Driver, but we know he never will.

"We stop elsewhere too, at farm crossings and stiles, where paths lead to lonely houses. Rheneas and I know all the places very well indeed, and our Driver used to say that we would stop even if he didn't put on the brakes!

"Sometimes, on Market Day, Ruth, Jemima, and Lucy were so full of people that the Guard would allow third-class passengers to travel in Agnes. She didn't like that at all, and would grumble. 'First —— class —— coach —— third —— class —— people.'

"That made me cross. 'Shut up,' I'd say, 'or I'll bump you!' That soon stopped her rudeness to my friends."

Just then some workmen came. "We're going to mend you now, Edward," they said. "Come along."

"Goodbye, Skarloey. Thank you for telling me about your Railway. It's a lovely little line."

"It is! It is! Thank you for talking to me, Edward. You've cheered me up. Goodbye!"

Skarloey watched Edward being taken back to the Works; then, shutting his eyes, he dozed in the warm afternoon sun. He smiled as he dozed, for he was dreaming, as old engines will, of happy days in the past.

Sir Handel

THE NEW ENGINES looked very smart. One was called Sir Handel, and the other Peter Sam.

"What a small shed!" grumbled Sir Handel. "This won't do at all!"

"I think it's nice," said Peter Sam.

"Huh!" grunted Sir Handel. "What's that rubbish?"

"Sh sh!" said Peter Sam, "that's Skarloey, the famous old engine.

"I'm sorry, Skarloey," he whispered, "Sir Handel's upset now, but he's quite nice really."

Skarloey felt sorry for Peter Sam.

"Now Sir Handel," said the Fireman next morning, "we'll get you ready."

"I'm tired," he yawned, "let Peter Sam go, he'd love it."

"No," said the Fireman, "Owner's orders, you're first."

"Oh well!" said Sir Handel sulkily, "I suppose I must."

When his driver arrived, Sir Handel puffed away to fetch the coaches.

"Whatever next?" he snorted. "Those aren't coaches; they're cattle trucks!"

"Oooooh!" screamed Agnes, Ruth, Lucy, Jemima, and Beatrice, "what a horrid engine!"

"It's not what I'm used to," clanked Sir Handel rebelliously, making for the station.

He rolled to the platform just as Gordon arrived.

"Hullo!" he said. "Who are you?"

"I'm Gordon. Who are you?"

"I'm Sir Handel. Yes, I've heard of you; you're an express engine I believe. So am I, but I'm used to bogie coaches, not these cattle trucks. Do you have bogie coaches? Oh yes, I see you do. We must have a chat sometime. Sorry I can't stop; must keep time, you know."

And he puffed off, leaving Gordon at a loss for words!

"Come along! COME ALONG!" he puffed.

"Cattle trucks! CATTLE TRUCKS!" grumbled the coaches. "We'll pay him out! WE'LL PAY HIM OUT!"

Presently they stopped at a station. The line curved here and began to climb. It was not very steep, but the day was misty, and the rails were slippery.

"Hold back!" whispered Agnes to Ruth. "Hold back!" whispered Ruth to Jemima. "Hold back!" whispered Jemima to Lucy. "Hold back!" whispered Lucy to Beatrice, and they giggled as Sir Handel started and their couplings tightened.

"Come on! COME ON!" he puffed as his wheels slipped on the greasy rails, "Comeon comeon COMEON COMEON!"

His wheels were spinning, but the coaches pulled him back, and the train stopped on the hill beyond the station.

"I can't do it, I can't do it," he grumbled, "I'm used to sensible bogie coaches, not these bumpy cattle trucks."

The Guard came up. "I think the coaches are up to something," he told the Driver. So they decided to bring the train down again to a level piece of line, to give Sir Handel a good start.

The Guard helped the Fireman put sand on the rails, and Sir Handel made a tremendous effort. The coaches tried hard to drag him back; but he puffed and pulled so hard that they were soon over the top and away on their journey.

The Thin Controller was severe with Sir Handel that night.

"You are a Troublesome Engine," he said. "You are rude, conceited, and much too big for your wheels. Next time I shall punish you severely."

Sir Handel was impressed, and behaved well for several days!

Then one morning he took the train to the top station. He was cross; it was Peter Sam's turn, but the Thin Controller had made him go instead.

"We'll leave the coaches," said his Driver, "and fetch some trucks from the Quarry."

"Trucks!" snorted Sir Handel, "TRUCKS!"

"Yes," his Driver repeated, "Trucks."

Sir Handel jerked forward; "I won't!" he muttered, "so there!" He lurched, bumped, and stopped. His Driver and Fireman got out.

"Told you!" said Sir Handel triumphantly.

He had pushed the rails apart, and settled down between them.

They telephoned the Thin Controller. He came up at once with Peter Sam, and brought some workmen in a truck. Then he and the Fireman took Peter Sam home with the coaches, while the Driver and workmen put Sir Handel back on the rails.

Sir Handel did not feel so pleased with himself when he crawled home, and found the Thin Controller waiting for him. "You are a very naughty engine," he said sternly. "You will stay in the Shed till I can trust you to behave."

Peter Sam and the Refreshment Lady

As Sir Handel was shut up, Peter Sam had to run the line. He was excited, and the Fireman found it hard to get him ready.

"Sober up, can't you!" he growled.

"Anybody would think", said Sir Handel rudely, "that he *wanted* to work."

"All *respectable* engines do," said Skarloey firmly. "I wish I could work myself. Keep calm, Peter Sam, don't get excited, and you'll do very well."

But Peter Sam was in such a state that he couldn't listen.

When his Driver came, Peter Sam ran along to fetch the coaches. "Peep pip pip peep! Come along girls!" he whistled, and although he was so excited, he remembered to be careful. "That's the way, my dears, gently does it."

"What did he say?" asked Jemima who was deaf.

"He said 'Come along, girls,' and he . . . he called us his dears," simpered the other coaches. "Really one does not know *what* to think . . . . . . such a handsome young engine too . . . . *so* nice and well mannered." And they tittered happily together as they followed Peter Sam.

Peter Sam fussed into the station to find Henry already there.

"This won't do, youngster," said Henry. "*I* can't be kept waiting. If you are late tonight, I'll go off and leave your passengers behind."

"Pooh!" said Peter Sam; but secretly he was a little worried.

But he couldn't feel worried for long.

"What fun it all is," he thought as he ran round his train.

He let off steam happily while he waited for the Guard to blow his whistle and wave his green flag.

Peter Sam puffed happily away, singing a little song. "I'm Peter Sam! I'm running this line! I'm Peter Sam! I'm running this line!"

The people waved as he passed the farms and cottages, and he gave a loud whistle at the School. The children all ran to see him puffing by.

Agnes, Ruth, Jemima, Lucy, and Beatrice enjoyed themselves too. "He's cocky . . . . trock trock . . . . but he's nice . . . . trock, trock; he's cocky . . . . trock trock . . . . but he's nice . . . . trock, trock," they sang as they trundled along. They were growing very fond of Peter Sam.

Every afternoon they had to wait an hour at the station by the Lake.

The Driver, Fireman, and the Guard usually bought something from the Refreshment Lady, and went and sat in Beatrice. The Refreshment Lady always came home on this train.

Time passed slowly today for Peter Sam.

At last his Driver and Fireman came. "Peep peeeeeep! Hurry up, please!" he whistled to the passengers, and they came strolling back to the station.

Peter Sam was sizzling with impatience. "How awful," he thought, "if we miss Henry's train."

The last passengers arrived. The Guard was ready with his flag and whistle. The Refreshment Lady walked across the platform.

Then it happened! . . .

The Guard says that Peter Sam was too impatient; Peter Sam says he was sure he heard a whistle. . . . Anyway, he started.

"Come quickly, come quickly!" he puffed.

"Stop! . . . Stop! . . . STOP!" wailed the coaches. "You've . . . left . . . her . . . behind . . . ! YOU'VE . . . LEFT . . . HER . . . BEHIND . . . !"

The Guard whistled and waved his red flag. The Driver, looking back, saw the Refreshment Lady shouting and running after the train.

"Bother!" groaned Peter Sam as he stopped. "We'll miss Henry now." The Refreshment Lady climbed into Beatrice, and they started again. "We're sure to be late! We're sure to be late!" panted Peter Sam frantically. His Driver had to keep checking him. "Steady, old boy, steady."

"Peep peep!" Peter Sam whistled at the stations. "Hurry! please hurry!" and they reached the big station just as Henry steamed in.

"Hurrah!" said Peter Sam, "we've caught him after all," and he let off steam with relief. "Whooooosh!"

"Not bad, youngster," said Henry loftily.

The Refreshment Lady shook her fist at Peter Sam. "What do you mean by leaving me behind?" she demanded.

"I'm sorry, Refreshment Lady, but I was worried about our passengers," and he told her what Henry had said.

The Refreshment Lady laughed. "You silly engine!" she said, "Henry wouldn't dare go; he's *got* to wait. It's a *guaranteed connection*!"

"Well!" said Peter Sam, "Well! Where's that Henry?"

But Peter Sam was too late that time, for Henry had chortled away!

Old Faithful

SIR HANDEL stayed shut up for several days. But one market day, Peter Sam could not work; he needed repairs.

Sir Handel was glad to come out. He tried to be kind, but the coaches didn't trust him. They were awkward and rude. He even sang them little songs; but it was no use.

It was most unfortunate, too, that Sir Handel had to check suddenly to avoid running over a sheep.

"He's bumped us!" screamed the coaches. "Let's pay him out!"

The coaches knew that all engines must go carefully at a place near the big station. But they were so cross with Sir Handel that they didn't care what they did. They surged into Sir Handel, making him lurch off the line. Luckily no one was hurt.

Sir Handel limped to the shed. The Thin Controller inspected the damage. "No more work for you today," he said. "Bother those coaches! We must take the village people home, and fetch the tourists, all without an engine."

"What about me, Sir?" said a voice.

"Skarloey!" he exclaimed, "can you do it?"

"I'll try," answered the old engine.

The coaches stood at the platform. Skarloey advanced on them hissing crossly. "I'm ashamed of you," he scolded, "such behaviour; you might have hurt your passengers. On Market Day too!"

"We're sorry, Skarloey, we didn't think; it's that Sir Handel, he's . . ."

"No tales," said Skarloey firmly, "I won't have it, and don't you dare try tricks on me."

"No Skarloey, of course not Skarloey," quavered the coaches meekly.

Skarloey might be old, and have dirty paint, but he was certainly an engine who would stand no nonsense.

His friends crowded round, and the Guard had to "shoo" them away before they could start. Skarloey felt happy; he remembered all the gates and stiles where he had to stop, and whistled to his friends. The sun shone, the rails were dry. "This is lovely," he thought.

But presently they began to climb, and he felt short of steam.

"Bother my tubes!" he panted.

"Take your time, old boy," soothed his Driver.

"I'll manage, I'll manage," he wheezed; and, pausing for "breath" at the stations, he gallantly struggled along.

After a rest at the top station, Skarloey was ready to start.

"It'll be better downhill," he thought.

The coaches ran nicely, but he soon began to feel tired again. His springs were weak, and the rail-joints jarred his wheels.

Then with a crack, a front spring broke, and he stopped.

"I feel all crooked," he complained.

"That's torn it," said his Driver, "we'll need a 'bus now for our passengers."

"No!" pleaded Skarloey, "I'd be ashamed to have a 'bus take my passengers. I'll get home or burst," he promised bravely.

The Thin Controller looked at his watch, and paced the platform. James and his train waited impatiently too.

They heard a hoarse "Peep Peep", then groaning, clanging, and clanking, Skarloey crept into sight. He was tilted to one side, and making fearful noises, but he plodded bravely on.

"I'll *do* it, I'll *do* it," he gasped between the clanks and groans, "I'll . . . I've done it!" and he sighed thankfully as the train stopped where James was waiting.

James said nothing. He waited for his passengers, and then respectfully puffed away.

"You were right, Sir," said Skarloey to the Owner that evening, "old engines can't pull trains like young ones."

The Owner smiled. "They can if they're mended, Old Faithful," he said, "and that's what will happen to you, you deserve it."

"Oh, Sir!" said Skarloey happily.

Sir Handel is longing for Skarloey to come back. He thinks Skarloey is the best engine in the world. He does his fair share of the work now, and the coaches never play tricks on him because he always manages them in "Skarloey's way".

If you have enjoyed these stories, you will enjoy a visit to the Tal-y-llyn Railway at Towyn in Wales.

The Rev. W. Awdry Railway Series

POP-UP BOOKS

Eight titles now available with paper mechanics by Roy Laming and pictures by Clive Spong.

Thomas the Tank Engine Goes Fishing
Bertie the Bus and Thomas the Tank Engine
Henry the Green Engine Gets Out
The Flying Kipper and Henry the Green Engine
James the Red Engine and the Troublesome Trucks
Thomas the Tank Engine and the Tractor
Percy the Small Engine Takes the Plunge
Henry the Green Engine and the Elephant

MAP OF THE ISLAND OF SODOR

Sodor, situated between Barrow-in-Furness and the Isle of Man is where Thomas, Henry, James, Edward, Gordon and the other engines have their adventures. This colourful map, measuring 560 × 760 mm when open, makes an excellent wall decoration. There is a key to many of the places where incidents in the books take place.